Written by **Angela Abbat**

Illustrated by **Josh McGill**

Shaya's Worries

ISBN 978-1-7774220-0-4

For my daughter and son, you are the loves of my life.

For Chloe, our precious pandemic Poodle whose constant love, companionship, and joy I could not repay.

For Lulu and Sparky, who melt my heart daily, and complete the trilogy of the Pups on the Pier.

To The Shipyards and the city of North Vancouver, for surrounding me in your beauty each and every day.

And to all the children out there, there's nothing to fear, when you share your feelings like Pups on the Pier.

MEET ANGELA ABBATE

Artist. Author. Advocate for mental health.

"Shaya's Worries" is a children's book created by a concerned mother to help young readers understand anxiety.

This Inaugural Book of the Pups on the Pier series is a pivotal step in what has already been an empowering journey for author Angela Abbate who has been outspoken about her own personal battle with anxiety. Afraid of dogs as a child, Angela has raved on the positive effects of getting her first puppy which has led to an undeniable passion of sharing her therapeutic experiences with dogs to the world. Pups on the Pier was created by Angela to raise awareness, create mindfulness, share solutions, inspire kindness (especially to yourself!), and offer information for others to safely enjoy the endless benefits of the remarkable creatures that changed her life.

MEET CHLOE

An 8-month-old Miniature Toy Poodle who believes she is
a princess even while running into glass doors or barfing in
the car. Her favorite foods include ice cream, peanut butter
smoothies, and socks. In the few hours a day she ISN'T
napping in weird spots, you can find Chloe showing off in
one of her many fabulous rhinestone dresses, power walk-
ing along the ocean, chewing on scrunchies, listening to
pop music, and watching sunsets with her mom on the pier.

MEET LULU

A 1-year-old Teacup Pomeranian who keeps her fabulous, fluffy figure by chasing golfcarts and biting ankles. She is a big fan of massages and soap operas, even if she can't always stay awake for her favorite ones. Her daddy is a rapper but she prefers European techno. This feisty pup is very picky about the pairs of shoes she chooses to destroy… according to Lulu, the "expensive ones just taste better." Lulu loves taking selfies, dancing in tutus, shopping for high-end fashion, and long walks on the sea wall. Lulu may be a diva, but all it takes is feeding her kabobs in the sunshine and you've got a loyal friend for life!

MEET SPARKY

A 9-year-old Jack Russel Pomeranian Mix, Sparky has both the wisdom and grumpiness of an older dog. A firm believer in consistency, he brushes his teeth every morning and eats his chicken and rice every night. This pup at heart listens to rap music and reggatone to pump himself up for a long day of chasing squirrels. However, Sparky rests as hard as he plays and enjoys sitting in yellow chairs, watching football, crossword puzzles, and getting spoiled at Gramma's. He is honored to be a self-appointed chief of the fun police, but his main role will always be loyal protector of all the humans and puppies he loves so dearly.

Shaya looked out at the pier,

Then to the ocean, her biggest fear.

Mom hugged her and said,

"Maybe we'll go to the pool today instead?"

Shaya nodded and got ready to go,

But big brother Sam cried, "No, no, no!"

"We never get to swim in the sea,"

He said, "And that's more fun for me."

Young Sam didn't understand his sister was scared,

If she told him that, he would have cared.

He would have tended to her broken heart,

Instead he said, "Shaya's dumb and smells like farts."

Mom watched as Shaya cried and started to shake,

Worried feelings can be a lot for a kid to take.

Every day got a little worse that summer,

Sam complained that Shaya was a total bummer,

But Mom knew it was something more,

Something keeping her favorite girl on the shore.

Fear of the unknown can make you very nervous,

She thought Shaya needed a friend… a purpose.

Mom knew what would brighten up her world,

The same thing that worked for her when she was a young girl…

One morning as the sun rose to fill the sky,

Shaya woke up and rubbed her eyes,

She looked and saw at the edge of the bed,

A tiny poodle, a new best friend.

Shaya squealed and cheered with glee,

"I can't believe you got me a puppy!"

Shaya loved her beige fur, fluffy and curly,

Sam came in and say, "Ahhh man, that dog is so girly!"

Sam might have thought the puppy was lame,

But the fact was she needed a name,

Sam wanted to call her Joey,

But Shaya wanted something prettier… how about Chloe?

Sam wondered if he would ever get his way,

But something great happened that day,

Shaya wanted to take the pup for a run,

And thought the pier by the ocean could be fun…

Sam grabbed Shaya by the hand and said, "Let's go!"

Mom watched from the upstairs window,

Shaya loved Chloe's little pink rhinestone leash,

And couldn't wait to show her off at the beach.

But when they got to the pier, Chloe let out a little bark,

She wanted to go to the grassy dog park.

Shaya let her go and Chloe ran up to some mutts,

And introduced herself… by sniffing their butts.

"Hi, I'm Chloe, so nice to meet you!"

The Pomeranian yipped, "Hi, I'm Lulu!"

But the Jack Russell mix was a little snarky,

He snarled and snipped, "Yo, I'm Sparky."

Chloe liked her new friends so asked for help,

She said, "I'm just a puppy, still learning to yelp."

"I'm scared of everything but don't want to say,

Because I love my new person and I want to stay"

Chloe was embarrassed but had to continue,

"If you're not always happy, will they get rid of you?"

Lulu nuzzled Chloe, while Sparky leaned in close,

"You have to share your feelings with the ones you love most."

Chloe understood but still didn't know how,

Sparky said when he was scared, he would let out a growl.

Since dogs can't talk, they find other ways to explain,

Like the way Lulu hides when she's scared of the rain.

Chloe thanked her new friends for the advice,

She thought the pups on the pier were super nice,

She ran back to Shaya and got a big hug!

When her leash was back on, she gave it a tug,

As soon as her tiny paws hit the hot sand,

She started to tremble, would Shaya understand?

Shaya sat down and held Chloe tight,

She whispered, "There, there. It will be alright."

"We don't have to do anything you don't want to do,"

Shaya said, "Besides, I'm scared of the ocean too."

Sam dove in the ocean and pretended like he was a shark,

Chloe got worried and started to bark.

It didn't matter that she wasn't brave,

She had her new little boy to save.

Chloe ran out of Shaya's arms and jumped in,

But the tiny poodle didn't know how to swim!

Chloe went under the water and she started to sink,

But she was back above the surface before she could blink,

What happened was perfectly clear,

Shaya learned how love conquers fear.

She saw Chloe suffer and had to scram,

To rescue Chloe like she tried to rescue Sam.

Shaya didn't think about herself, not at that hour,

That's when a little girl learned she had big power.

Sam saw his sister's fear and finally understood,

She would play in the ocean if she could,

He promised no more teasing, no more messing,

He asked if she and Chloe wanted a lesson.

He taught her how to be careful with the tide,

And how fun boogie boards were to ride.

He held Chloe while she learned about the ocean's waves and flows,

She was so grateful she licked him right on the nose!

Mom had been watching her children play so sweet,

And she brought them down a picnic to eat,

Shaya said she wasn't ready to go just yet,

So, they ate the picnic while they watched the sunset.

Mom, Sam, and Shaya makes three,

But Chloe made them a family.

As the sun went down and the stars came out,

Shaya finally understood what courage was about.

"I know Chloe was supposed to make me feel calm,"

Shaya whispered, "But I really like being her mom."

They hugged each other and looked out at the sea,

Moms know taking care of others can bring great peace.

Sam said all the talk about feelings was making him bored,

So, the family packed up and left the shore.

They decided to take one last look on the pier,

To see if Chloe's new friends might appear....

Sure enough, on the dock wearing her little tutu,

Strutting around was the pier princess, Lulu.

Sam was ready to throw in the towel,

But then heard the rumble of Sparky's low growl.

Sparky was tough and puffed out his chest,

Sam did the same, he'd show him who's best!

Mom stepped and said, "Sam, he's afraid."

So, Sam knelt down and a friendship was made.

Sam reached in his pocket for freeze dried meat,

Sparky's eyes grew big and he drooled at the treat,

Sam asked his mom if it was okay,

But before she said, "Yes," Sparky had his own way,

He jumped up and grabbed the snack in midair,

Sam screamed, "Dang, dog, I was planning to share."

Sparky swallowed it whole which gave him a laugh,

Then he licked Sam's face with a doggy kiss bath.

It was all Mom could do to drag Sam from the pier,

He cried out, "No, my new best friend lives here."

As Sam thought he would forever wallow in sorrow,

Shaya said, "We could always come back tomorrow."

"You mean it?" he said with tears in his eyes,

Shaya really did, much to her surprise.

"I didn't think I'd like the ocean, but I do,"

She smiled, "And I had fun spending the day with you."

Chloe was happy everything seemed just right,

But something happened when she curled up that night,

She looked around and everything was pitch black,

She opened her mouth and started to yap.

Shaya came running to check on her pup,

She saw she was shaking and picked her right up,

Shaya held her close and kissed her tiny head,

"Come, Chloe, you can sleep in my bed."

Chloe climbed in, oh the covers she would steal,

She learned it helps to say how you feel,

It lets other know you need some care,

Whether it's from worries or scares,

Sometimes we feel bad and don't know why,

That's okay too and it's okay to cry.

Chloe and Shaya needed each other,

Just like Shaya needed her big brother.

It turned out Sam could be pretty sweet,

And the poodle who made their family complete,

Showed everyone what it meant to stand tall,

But the greatest lesson for all…

For Sparky, Lulu, and Chloe,

For Mom, Sam, and Shaya,

Was there's nothing to fear,

When you share your feelings like Pups on the Pier.

Manufactured by Amazon.ca
Bolton, ON